SEJAL

The Walk for Water

SEJAL
The Walk for Water

Brad Pauquette

www.ColumbusPressBooks.com

Columbus Press
P.O. Box 91028
Columbus, OH 43209
www.ColumbusPressBooks.com

Cover Artwork & Design
Columbus Publishing Lab
www.ColumbusPublishingLab.com

Print ISBN 978-0-9891737-7-3
Ebook ISBN 978-0-9891737-8-0

Printed in the United States of America
1 3 5 7 9 10 8 6 4 2

"The poor and needy search for water,
but there is none;
their tongues are parched with thirst.
But I the Lord will answer them;
I, the God of Israel, will not forsake them.
I will make rivers flow on barren heights,
and springs within the valleys.
I will turn the desert into pools of water...
so that people may see and know,
may consider and understand,
that the hand of the Lord has done this,
that the Holy One of Israel has created it.
Isaiah 41:17-20

To Pastor Stephen.
I love him because he first loved me.

I

I sit on a rock in front of my hut. It is early in the afternoon, and the Indian sun shines down from high in the sky. I look out over my village, Muthuramapuram, and I smile at the longhouses and grass covered huts lining the road that passes through our village. Almost six hundred people live in this village, and it feels like a rock has been lifted from our shoulders. Everyone feels it, even a silly girl, it's infectious.

The air smells different than it did yesterday. There is less sweat caked under our clothes today, even though the day is just as hot. Instead of the putrid onion and garlic smell of tired bodies, the sweet smell of the banana trees wafts down the village road. Instead of sticking to me, my sari drifts delicately around me in the occasional waft of breeze, and it hugs my torso, lean and firm.

An old man passes along the road in front of me. Uncle Raj wears a dusty sarong that falls all the way to his ankles. His dirty brown feet kick out from underneath with each step. Though he does not yet use a cane, he walks in quick two-step bursts. Left-right, and then the left takes its time making its way back to the front. He fancies himself for a yogi, with his long white beard and eyes that always seem to be half-asleep, and the long hours he spends idling in front of the village temple each day. Normally, I would scurry away when he passes, or pretend to be mending my sandal. On days before this one he would scowl at me, shout that I was a curse to my house, and tell my father to beat me for lazing on a rock in the middle of the afternoon. But today, his lips turn up into what I must assume is his smile, I've never seen one before, and he bows his head towards the ground just slightly. He continues to shuffle past, and my eyes fall to the ground.

For the first afternoon that I can remember, the brilliant brown hue of the skin on my ankles and feet is not caked with dusty residue and mud. I look at my hands, and my pink and white fingernails sparkle in the light of the afternoon sun, dancing and winking at me.

In days past in the village, all of our saris were off-white, hanging limp off of our shoulders. But today, as the women pass, each one walks with her head held high above her clothing, each in brilliant mustard, chartreuse, rose, and violet, our garments hovering around us, fluttering along like royal gowns.

For the first time I can remember in fourteen years, I have a moment to rest in the afternoon. I raise my arms above my head and feel my spine elongate towards the sky, my back arching like a bamboo reed in the spring winds.

I am alone, but still I try to stifle a giggle that begins deep in my chest and escapes from between my ivory teeth. "Sejal," I whisper to myself. "Your hands are beautiful."

Manisha, who lives in the hut next to me, looks up at me from her walk home, a bundled sack of groceries from the village market atop her head. Her teeth peek out from behind her lips, and her eyes brighten when they meet mine.

"What's so funny, sister?" she chides, grinning and wrinkling her nose at me. We are not any more related than anyone else in the village, but today I wish she was my older sister. We could cook together in the afternoon, and when my father came home, he would smile at us, and tell us that he loved us. At night, we would sit around a small fire together and he would tell us stories about our mother.

Perhaps tonight, when my father comes home he will smile at me. Perhaps he'll change into his other shirt, and we'll laugh about Uncle Raj's beard and draw cartoons in the dirt.

"Sejal," perhaps he will tell me, "you look just like your mother." And then I'll smile, and then I'll cry, and he'll hold me, and tell me how happy he is to have me. When it's late and I go into the hut to go to sleep, he'll come over to where I'm lying, squeeze my shoulder and tell me to have sweet dreams, that tomorrow's a new day. I'll fall asleep quickly, remembering the warmth of his hand on my shoulder and the smell of his skin, and for just a moment I'll be able to remember what my mother looked like in the dusk when she would wrap the blanket around me, sing me a lullaby and kiss my forehead.

"Ninnie baba ninnie," *Sleep baby sleep*, she'll whisper into my ear, and her cheek will brush over mine.

It has been eight years since my mother died, and in all of that time this night that plays in my mind has never happened. But today is the most different day I have ever had.

Yesterday began like all of the days before it.

II

"Sejal!" my father had barked, as he stepped out of our hut into the darkness of early morning. He didn't wait to see if I would get up. He knew I would.

I sat up and rubbed the sleep from my eyes. I massaged my feet and rubbed the dead skin from between my toes before I slid them into my sandals.

When I came outside, my father was already a hundred meters down the road to the west, walking quickly with his back to me. He does not bounce when he walks, the mass of his body simply moves in a straight line down his path, his feet attacking and retreating underneath of him with each step. For five kilometers each way his body simply drives forward, autonomously hovering above the ground atop his rotating legs.

It was still dark, and most days it is dark again before he returns from the sorghum fields. Most days, he brings home a small bag of sorghum grain, and if he's lucky, a few coins will jingle in his pocket.

Sorghum—we eat it, they feed it to the goats and the chickens, and I once heard my father tell Uncle Raj they can even burn it to run trucks. Uncle Raj just closed his eyes and shook his head, as if he might charm the idea from the universe.

Once, I asked my father what he does at the farm, but he only shook his head.

"I load a truck," he finally explained. "The women and the old men drag the burlap sacks in. We combine them and load them onto the truck."

"Where does the truck go?" I asked him.

"I don't know, Sejal," he sighed. "Away to someone who can buy the bags I suppose. I just load the truck."

"What women?"

"Huh?"

"The women who bring the sacks. Who are they?"

"I don't know, Sejal. I've never asked," he kneaded his brow with his right hand. "From another village, I suppose."

"But then who gets their water?" I was perplexed.

"No more questions, Sejal."

This was more than my father normally said to me in a week.

"Do they get paid?"

My father shrugged, nodded, stood up and walked away from me.

Yesterday, I stood outside of our hut and rubbed the cold from my arms, looking away from my father towards a sliver of the sun peeking over the hillside. Behind our hut, atop a large rock, a small pot of water remained from the day before. I went over and cupped my hands, but before I could plunge them into the water, I saw *them* shimmering in the dawn light. The water teemed with wriggling larvae.

I breathed deeply and sighed. Mosquitoes.

I threw the contents of the water pot into the dirt, and stamped my foot.

"Come on slow-poke," Manisha called out from behind me. "Time to go."

I turned around. She carried her empty water jar under her arm. Manisha's skin was darker than mine, almost black like an African, even more so in the putrid light of dawn. Her golden Lakshmi bracelet twinkled in the soft light. It was a gift from her husband that she said would encourage the Goddess Lakshmi to bless their house with a child. She had polished it again that morning. She polishes it every morning. If Lakshmi's blessing came as a result of polishing, their house would be stacked with children in every corner.

I know I should have said good morning, but I was thirsty and my face felt grotty, so I only grunted, plucked my water jar from the doorway of my hut and joined her in the road.

Manisha smiled at me, and turned to head west, in the direction my father had gone.

"Where are you going?" I asked her.

"To the stream, where do you think?" Manisha used her voice that always seems to be arguing. Of course, to me, before the sun was over the hillside, every voice sounded like it was arguing.

"Huh? Why don't we just go to the pool, like yesterday, it's only four kilometers. The stream is like six."

"My water was alive this morning, Sejal. So was yours. I saw you throw it out. We shouldn't have gone there yesterday. It's been too long since the rains. Don't be stupid."

"I'm not stupid," I threw back at her. "And it wasn't that bad, it wasn't even cloudy yet, you idiot."

She glared at me. Her black eyes didn't move from mine.

"Do what you want, but your father will beat you if you bring home that stink-hole water, Sejal."

I glared back at her and huffed.

"Sejal, you may not be old enough to know, but look down the village, all of the women are headed west, toward the stream. Nobody's coming this way."

"Sounds like you better catch up then," I shouted at her.

"Isn't six kilometers with me better than four by yourself?"

"I guess I'll find out," I snapped back. "You better get going."

"Sejal, you shouldn't go alone anyway. It's not safe to go alone."

"I don't care if you're older, I've still been carrying water more years than you! I'll decide where I get it."

"Sejal, your jar will be more mud than water when you get it back home—"

"Shut up!" I yelled at her, and stormed off to the east, towards the pool.

III

The pool is only there for part of the year. After the rainy season ends and the water runs off of the mountains, it collects in a basin at the bottom of the foothills. For a time, the water runs through the basin, in and out of the thirsty ravines that have formed in the cracked, dry earth. But a couple of weeks after the rain, the water level drops, and it sits stagnant in the basin, waiting to evaporate.

The water stopped flowing four days ago, but it was still deeper than my knees and clear the day before. I stormed off towards the pond alone, my brow furrowed against the brightening sun in front of me, and against Manisha's insolence.

The dust turned into more dust in front of me, kicking up in tiny sand storms, assaulting my toes with every step. The roadway was deserted except for the truck headed towards the village with produce and cans of gasoline. It will stop at the market and continue on to the next village, and on to the next.

I picked my way along the road of beaten earth with my water jar under my arm, muttering to myself.

"She is not my mother." I complained to myself.

"She is only five years older than me, and she's only been married for two," I pronounced to no one as I kicked a pebble along in front of me. "Two years and no child. Lakshmi sees her bracelet, Manisha makes sure everyone sees her stupid bracelet, but still no child."

The sun beat down upon me by the time I approached the watering hole. The broken yellow grass gave way to tall green reeds in the distance, and I knew I was getting close.

As I parted the reeds, I saw them and my heart sank.

Two water buffalo stood in the middle of the watering hole, the water barely three inches above their hooves. One of them turned to me and snorted, its glassy eyes scarcely registering me, its tail flicking gnats and flies from its back.

The two stood there, side by side, and their feces, greasy green globs, dripped down their hind legs and into the murky water with metronome consistency. The hole was scarcely twelve feet across, and they chewed on the reeds on the edge of the pool, their teeth constantly grating while the excrement trickled out their back ends.

I looked down at the water, it was mud. Manisha was right, I would fill my water jar, and on the walk home the debris would settle out. My fifteen liter jar would be four liters of mud.

I wanted to scream. I wanted to throw my jar to the ground. I wanted to charge at the water buffalo and hit them with a stick. I wanted to call out and curse Shiva and the ground and the sun. I wanted to curse my village and Manisha, and then break my jar on the rock.

The more I thought about it, the more I wanted to scream and shout and beat the ground with my fist and shout obscenities at the water buffalo. Then when I was done, I would curl into a ball on the edge of the watering hole, gaze listlessly out over the murky water, and wait for the sun to go down.

But I didn't do any of those things, because I was still Sejal. So I sighed into the atmosphere loud enough for the gods to hear me, turned around and began my walk back towards the village.

More than anything else, I wanted a drink of water.

IV

Today, the sun is hot on my rock, so I walk to the basin behind our hut, cup my hands and plunge them into the clear water. I take a long drink from my hands, and the water is sweet and cold. I could use the cup, but it's so clean I feel like I should never use it again.

I splash a bit of the water on my face, and my skin, heated by the hot Indian sun, drinks it in. The excess rolls down my cheeks and onto my neck, and evaporates from the collar of my tunic instantaneously.

I take another drink and savor the water in my mouth before I swallow it. When I am finished, I pat my hands dry on my sari, and bend over to step inside of our hut where, despite the absence of the scorching sun, the air is hot and dry.

Yesterday, it was past nine o'clock before I passed by the hut on my way back from the watering hole. I had followed my lone footprints all the way back to the village as the sun had risen higher in the sky, until I imagined that the dust kicked up by each step was sucked directly into my throat, coating the back of my mouth. By the time I reached the village, I had forgotten even to care that I was thirsty.

As I walked past my hut, I remembered my conversation with Manisha that morning, and I shook my head. It would only be so long before I met her; she would be coming back from the stream with a jar full of water, feeling refreshed and chatting animatedly with the older women from the village. But I would be parched and grumpy, just as I had been a few hours earlier.

I knew that, undoubtedly, when she met me she would gloat. "How was the water?" she would chide me. "Enough to take a swim?"

I decided that I would ignore her. I had made a mistake, and Manisha would rub it in my face, but I was too tired to fight with her. Too thirsty to care.

On my way through the town, I passed the place where men had been working for a week. They had stopped several days before.

"They're from the city," my father answered me one night as we ate, after I had asked him four times. "They think they're helping us."

I sat and thought for awhile. Then finally I spoke. "They don't look like government men."

"They're not from the government, Sejal," he answered flatly. "If they were, they would know that they're wasting their time."

"But what are they doing?" I asked.

"No more questions, I'm too tired," he said and stood up. "Goodnight, Sejal."

"Please father," I pleaded. "What are they trying to do?"

"The same thing the government tried to do. Six times they tried," he answered defeatedly. "Don't get your hopes up, Sejal. Goodnight."

I went to bed after him, unaware of anything the government had tried to do for us six times.

But yesterday when I walked past, the men weren't working. A large concrete slab sat on the property of the man who owns the market, with yellow ropes encircling it. A rock, ten inches in diameter, sat in the center of the slab, like a shrine.

As I walked, I wondered what it could be. Something the government had failed, something they thought would help us. *Perhaps it is a shrine*, I thought, *perhaps it will help us.*

I walked onward towards the stream. I passed the tin-roofed market with the satellite dish affixed to the concrete block, I passed the village shrine to Shiva and walked past fifty more yards of grass-thatched huts and long wooden houses lining the road.

After I had passed through town and walked for another 45 minutes, I saw them in the distance. A dozen women together, each with a jar on their head. Manisha always held her jar on her head with her right hand positioned slightly higher than her left. Her lean figure grew as we approached each other.

V

As I drew closer to Manisha, who was returning from the stream with what I assumed was a full pitcher of water, I was determined not to look at her. I held my head high and looked straight down the road towards the next clump of women coming over the horizon with their water jars on their heads.

But she called out before I passed. "Sejal!"

I turned my head towards her as I passed her and wrinkled my nose.

"Sejal," she called again. "Don't go that way, it's too late."

I huffed loudly enough for her to hear, and kept walking. Her plastic water jar thumped deeply as she placed it on the ground, and she ran after me.

"Sejal," she pleaded from behind me and tugged on the shoulder of my sari. "Don't go that way. It's not safe. You can share my water. It's enough."

I laughed and kept walking.

"Sejal, please—"

"Why wouldn't I get my own water, Manisha?" I snapped back at her.

She ran around to the front of me and I stopped.

"You shouldn't ever go alone, your mother would have told you that," she began. "But especially not today. There were two men watching us by the stream. It's not safe alone."

I laughed again. "I'm not scared," I told her. "Go back to the village, Manisha, and leave me alone."

"Sejal," she pleaded. "Just share my water."

I waited for the trick, I searched her eyes for her angle, but I didn't find one. She bit her lower lip and her eyes glistened with moisture.

"Please, Sejal, just trust me."

I thought about what she said, then began walking towards the stream.

"Sejal always gets her own water," I told her. "Since I was six years old, every day I have gotten my own water. If you want to come with me, you can, but I'm going."

"But Sejal!" she shouted. "What about my water? It weighs 15 kilos, I'm not going to carry it all the way there and back again."

"Then dump it," I retorted. "You can fill it again and we'll carry our full jars together."

I heard her scurry back to her jar, and I snickered to myself. She wouldn't come. Manisha was trying to be my mother again, but she wouldn't follow through. In the end, I was on my own, just like always.

Then I heard the water splash into the dirt and I turned around to watch the liquid seep into the thirsty, cracked earth. Within moments the water was gone and even the mud was drying.

My mouth fell open and I held my hand to my throat. I nearly threw myself on the ground to drink from the mud, but instead I coughed twice, swallowed my spit and turned again to keep walking.

Manisha jogged to catch up with me, and together we set off for the stream.

VI

Manisha chattered as we walked along towards the stream. I would have held up my end of the conversation, or at least told her to shut up, but my mouth was too dry. She talked and talked, and all I could think about was the water from her jar seeping into the mud back near the village.

The sun continued to rise as we walked and it beat down on us with increasing intensity with each step. At first it felt like bugs were tickling my throat, but before long my throat just felt sticky.

At least Manisha's incessant need to blabber gave me something to focus on as we walked, instead of the way my tongue sometimes felt like it was caked with sand.

By the time we could see the trees that line the stream, the sun was high above us and my head had started to throb. At the point where we turned off the road to follow the beaten path through the field, into the trees surrounding the stream I broke off and sprinted towards the sound of the water flowing through the brook.

"Sejal!" Manisha called after me. "Sejal, why are you running?"

I dropped to my knees at the edge of the water, plunged my hands into the water and drank deeply. Over and over I plunged my hands into the water and drank until I felt like my esophagus was filled to the top and any more might spill back into my mouth. I knew my belly would hurt soon, but I didn't care. The stream was far, but the water was always cool.

Manisha finally caught up to me as I sat back on the bank and relaxed.

"Thirsty?" she asked me. "Why didn't you just drink some of my water before I dumped it out back at the village?"

I turned to her and glared. Then she laughed. Before long I laughed too.

We sat on the bank of the stream for a few minutes. We had both already walked more than 14 kilometers apiece that morning—hours in the hot sun. We had six more kilometers to go, a two hour trek with fifteen kilograms of water on each of our heads.

"You're right, Manisha," I goaded her and laughed. "The stream is lined with scary-looking men. Oh, I'm so scared."

"Just promise me you won't go this far from the village alone." Her eyes were full of concern. "So many things could happen."

"Right," I laughed. "What, like tigers? My father told me

that one too. Cobras?" I pretended my arm was a snake, hissed and pinched her arm. "I know about snakes and tigers, Manisha. Thanks."

"There are other things too, Sejal. Worse things…" she trailed off.

"Like what?"

"Like you could be taken. You don't believe it, but it happens," she told me. "Women from the villages disappear, and there's no one to look for them. You're so pretty—"

"Shut up, Manisha," I cut her off and laughed. "Is this the prank? Is this why you came out here with me, to scare me? My father would have told me if there were men who might snatch me."

"Your father never tells you anything, Sejal."

That shut me up. I turned away from her and swallowed hard.

"Sejal…" she placed her hand on my shoulder.

"OK, OK, Manisha. I promise. I won't go alone."

We sat in silence for a few minutes and listened to the water trickle over the stones in the stream.

"Come on, time to go," Manisha finally said, standing up and slapping me on the arm.

We dipped our jars into the stream to fill them up. First I filled my jar in the shallow stream, then she filled hers up and dumped some of it into mine to top me off. She filled hers as far as she could.

"Split the difference," I begged her.

"Second trip," she said, and laughed.

"Fine," and I playfully splashed her.

She gave me a look, smiled with all of her teeth and splashed me back.

Suddenly, a deep, masculine voice broke out over the sounds of the water.

"Girls," a man said from close behind us on the bank. "Need some help with your water?"

We both turned around and saw two men standing by the edge of the stream.

VII

The one who had spoken smiled.

The two men standing on the bank between us and the trail back to the road were dressed strangely. They wore light colored trousers with pockets, held up by thick leather belts, instead of the skirt-like sarongs worn by the men in our village. They wore western hats and sunglasses, and their skin was lighter than ours. Not as light as an American's, but lighter than the Indians in our village.

They both stood with their thumbs tucked into their belts, looking down at us. One of them had a machete strapped to his belt, while the taller one carried a satchel on his back.

"Girls?" the taller one spoke to us again and smiled. His teeth were remarkably straight and white. "We'd like to help you with your water."

I didn't know whether to speak. I didn't know whether

to ignore them or run away. So we stared until finally Manisha spoke. "No thank you sir, we were just leaving." She began to walk towards the bank.

The two men stepped closer together to completely block the path that led beyond the reeds and trees that surrounded the stream for ten yards. Beyond the trees was a grass field like all of the others we had walked past to get to the stream, and thirty yards into the field was the road.

"Excuse me, sir," she said and waited for them to part.

My belly began to burn with adrenaline, and my breathing quickened. I could feel sweat beads forming at my hairline and my palms were growing moist.

"No, I insist, your jar still has room," he told her as the smile faded and he licked his lips. The smile returned just as quickly. "Let me take you upstream, I can top off your jar."

"No, thank you sir," she politely said again, but I could hear her voice beginning to shake. "We don't wish to trouble you, sir."

The man took a step forward and grabbed her wrist. "It's no trouble," he said through clamped teeth. The skin puckered and instantly turned red around his grip. The taller man looked towards his partner and motioned his head towards me.

The man took a step towards me, reaching out with one hand and placing the other on the butt of his machete.

"Come along, then," he instructed, and waved with his

fingers for me to take his hand. "We'll just head downstream and top off your jars."

I bit my lower lip and looked at the ground. There was nowhere to run. The stream was surrounded by trees except for the path we had taken. I could run through the water for fifty yards or more before I found another break in the foliage. Besides, I couldn't leave Manisha.

I rubbed the palm of my free hand with my fingers and looked at his outstretched hand. His fingernails were clean, and I could smell him. He smelled like something artificial, like something one of the merchants might bring through our town.

Finally, I looked at Manisha, pleading with my eyes for an option, begging for a direction.

Manisha simply looked back at me with her large black eyes, and ever-so-slightly shook her head.

VIII

Manisha's eyes widened as I reached out towards the man with my left hand. She didn't see as my right hand tightened around the handle of my water jar. I reached out and grabbed his wrist, pulling him down towards me, then I swung my plastic water jar full of 15 kilograms of water as hard as I could.

The plastic cracked as it made contact with his forehead and water gushed out. He staggered backward and fell to the ground.

Before the other man could react, I charged the four steps to him and shoved the raw plastic shards of the cracked jar into his chin. He let go of Manisha to fend off the sharp plastic from his face and I drove my knee into his groin as hard as I could. The tall man doubled over, but still reached out for me as I grabbed Manisha and ran for the path.

"My jar!" she shouted and turned to look back.

"Leave it," I yelled back to her and yanked her wrist forward. We ran as fast as we could through the trees.

Manisha began to sob when we reached the trees.

"Slow down, slow down," she cried out as we ran.

"Not yet, we have to get to the road," I yelled back.

"Those men, were they…were they—" she called after me, she was slowing down and I could feel her growing heavier in my grasp.

"I don't know. I don't know anything." I continued to pull her forward to the road. As we neared it, I turned around and looked back towards her. "If they are, they're going to come after us, we have to keep going. We have to make it to the road. Let's go!"

"Sejal!" she tried to warn me.

I pulled as hard as I could, her hand slipped from my grasp and I went sprawling into the dirt road.

Manisha shrieked as a jeep slid to a halt, stopping just a few feet from where I lay in the road. I screamed. We could fetch water along this road for a week and never see another car. Of course when we were running from these men one would almost hit me.

I scrambled to my feet and for a moment thought I was meant to die that day. A man jumped out of the jeep.

He wore city clothes, but he was short and his skin was dark like Manisha's. He spoke to us first in Hindi and then in Marathi.

"Are you OK?" he clambered over to me. "You are a strange girl, jumping in the road," he laughed, and helped me to my feet. He tried to brush off my arms, but I withdrew.

"I'm sorry," he said, "are you OK?"

I just shook my head, ran to Manisha, buried my head in her sari and cried.

"It was an accident, you look fine," he pleaded. "Are you injured?"

I looked up and shook my head.

The man looked towards the woods then, and his smiling face fell. "Oh, sisters, you are from Muthuramapuram? Come in my jeep, I'm going there too."

I looked at Manisha and she shook her head. He nodded towards the trees this time, and we all looked. Two men were staggering along the path, nearly to the field. The tall man bled from his chin and limped along while the other held a rag, damp with blood to his forehead.

The man with the jeep looked directly at me, looked into my eyes and nodded as if he understood everything. There was something familiar about the man, even though I'd never seen him before, as if he knew about what had happened with the men by the stream, as if he knew about the walk that morning, as if he even knew about my mother.

I looked into his eyes, something I'd rarely ever done to a man before, and nodded my head.

"Come sisters," the man with the jeep said again. "We go now."

IX

The man looked over at the two of us as he drove.

"My name is Thomas," he finally said. I nodded and Manisha continued to stare off into the distance.

"You're lucky I was driving by," he said after another stretch of road had passed. "The world is full of violent men."

I folded my fingers and placed my hands in my lap, watching them vibrate as the jeep rattled along. I had never ridden in a car before, but the way the wind moved through my braided hair reminded me of my mother's hands, lingering over my braids before bedtime each night when I was a young girl.

"God-willing, soon you won't have to make that walk anymore," Thomas said to no one in particular, trying his hardest to avoid the holes that littered the roadway.

There was silence again, and his words hung ominously in the jeep. The wind rushed over our heads, and the diesel engine strained as we plodded over the terrain and unkempt roads. I watched the scenery whiz by, and I watched the man, how steadily he worked the controls.

Manisha stared at her hands and twirled her Lakshmi bracelet around her wrist. I didn't want to say anything to a man I didn't know, but I was so close to him in the middle of the front seat of the jeep, and he seemed to be waiting for one of us to say something. I could feel him listening, waiting for one of us to speak, and I knew Manisha never would.

"Sir?" I finally ventured. "My name is Sejal, and this is my neighbor, Manisha."

He nodded and continued to look ahead towards the road.

"Sir? Why won't we have to make that walk anymore?"

He smiled, but did not look at me. "Soon," he explained, "maybe tonight, you will have a well in your village, you will be able to walk to the place my men have been working and fill your jars."

I smiled. "Sir? My father said that men from the government have come six times before to do the same thing you're doing. Our village is cursed, sir. I'm sorry."

"Sejal?" he confirmed my name.

I nodded.

"It is not I who drills your well, it is the power of the Living God, Jesus." He smiled at me and I wrinkled my brow.

"You're right, when we drilled the well we found very little water where there should have been. We cleaned out the well and bored three times, but we still didn't find any water pressure."

He slowed down as we passed women threshing grain in the roadway, leaving the kernels out to be crushed by passing cars.

"But three days ago, Sejal, we covered the well with a rock. For those three days I went back to the city, and I have been praying. Together with my friends, we have been praying to God for this well to give you water. Today, Jesus will give you water, I know it." Thomas looked at me, and I could see his eyes smile through the dark tint on his glasses.

"My great aunt and uncle pray to Jesus," I told him. "They bought the prayer card from a brahman. They told me that you only pray to Jesus when you need help for something right away. But I don't think he could bring water to our village. It's too big a job for a little God like Jesus."

"We'll see, we'll see soon enough, child." He leaned forward to look past me, to speak to Manisha. "Has Lakshmi answered you?" he asked her, and nodded towards her bracelet.

She shook her head.

"Has Lakshmi spoken to you? Have you heard her voice?"

Manisha shook her head again and bit her lower lip. "No, sir."

"There is only one God who answers, Manisha," he told her.

Again, silence hung in the jeep and I listened to the wind whistle past my ears as Manisha considered Thomas's words.

"We'll see," she finally said with a smirk. I bit my lower lip to stifle my giggle, and then looked to the man to see if he would be mad. I held my breath hoping he wouldn't stop the car and force us to get out.

But instead, Thomas laughed. Then I giggled nervously beside him.

"Yes, Manisha," he told her. "You are right, we will see."

He laughed again and then silence fell over the jeep as the first huts of Muthuramapuram came into view. I should have felt happy. I was safe, I was alive, I was zooming towards my home in a car, a trek that would have taken me two hours on foot.

But I knew that I had no water. I had no water jar. Even if I got through the night, what would I do the next day? And the day after that would I carry water back to my hut in my hands? Even if there was a well in my village, which there wouldn't be, I had nothing but a bowl and a pot to put it in.

And my father would come over the horizon in a few hours, home from the fields with a bag of sorghum ready to be boiled, thirsty for a cool drink.

X

Thomas dropped us off in the middle of the village. The people at the market stared as we got out and walked off towards our homes.

It was late in the afternoon and I hadn't eaten yet, which wasn't unusual. But after walking for hours and then the events of the last hour, my stomach grumbled audibly as I approached the entrance to my hut. I keep a small store of chapati, our unleaved bread made more or less from sorghum and water, in a basket inside of the hut when I can, and there was a little left. I had made it the day before and it was dry and stale. But it was warm from sitting inside of the hut all day, so I closed my eyes as I pulled it from the basket and pretended it was fresh from an oven, not day-old out of a basket.

I had two pieces, so I went outside and took the other to Manisha. If I ate both, I would be too thirsty, and neither of us had any water for the evening meal.

"What are we going to do for water, Manisha?" I asked her as she graciously accepted the bread. I sat down beside her inside of her mud shack. It had two rooms, one just for sleeping. The mud walls and thatched roof kept it cooler than our one-room hut, which was made of stacked straw and mud.

It wasn't the first time one of the two of us had been without water, but it was the first time that neither of us had any. In times past, if one of our jars spilled on the way home or a rat got into the jar while it sat outside, we would share. Just so neither of us mentioned it, with any luck my father and her husband would never notice that we each only had a few liters.

"Your husband will be upset," I reminded her.

"And your father will beat you," she laughed. I didn't see the humor.

"So what's the plan? We could ask Mrs. Nayar."

"Yes, I'm sure she would love to split her jar three ways," Manisha scowled.

"Yah, but we would just need a little—"

"And what would we put it in, Sejal? Huh?" she cut me off.

I didn't know what to say. I knew my father kept a few coins underneath of the carved wooden temple in our hut, but I wasn't allowed to touch them. There probably weren't enough for a new water jar, and even if there were, he would know I had taken them.

"We'll just use a bowl or something," I told her. "At least we would have water. Our jars are gone, it's better to have water but no jar then no jar *and* no water."

"But what about tomorrow, and the day after, and the day after?" she asked.

I just shook my head. "Maybe when your husband comes home and my father is here, maybe together we'll have enough money for a new jar and we can share it until we can get a second one."

She bundled her legs up to herself, placed her head on her knees and sighed.

I reached out and grabbed her hand.

"Manisha?"

She looked at me.

"Thanks for going with me to the stream today."

She looked at me with misty eyes and nodded. I squeezed her hand, got up and hurried out.

XI

For an hour or more I hid in my hut, lying on my straw mattress and staring up at the ceiling. The day was finally cooling down as the sun stretched for the hills on the western horizon. Normally, I start sorghum soaking in a pot of water in the morning, and by the afternoon it's tender enough to boil and eat or crush into coarse flour for bread. But with no water yesterday morning, nothing was soaking.

On such a day without soaking grain, I could use a little oil to pop the sorghum into yawar—crunchy puffed kernels. But threshing the hard, dry grains for flour would be impossible if it hadn't been soaking all day. It would be a lean, parching meal without a cup of water to wash it down—if there was a meal for me at all.

I knew that when the sun finally reached the horizon, my father would come home and he would find me lying on my mat with no water and no food, and he would punish me. My father never yelled, even when he was angry. There would be no lecture, his words were as scarce in his fury as they were in his joy. All of his thoughts and lectures, all of his disappointment with me, all of his frustration with my constant failures to replace my mother would be explained in the tiny whistling wind that preceded the back of his hand.

Without any recourse, without hope, I lay on my bed looking at the tiny blades of straw that made up the ceiling. As I thought about the men at the river, as I thought about the water buffalo in the pool, as I thought about the water alive and teeming with mosquito larvae that morning, and as I thought about my mother, the straw above blurred into a shadowed nebula through the tears that filled my eyes.

First one hot tear rolled down my cheek, then another. As I considered them and the others that would follow that afternoon and in the days and weeks and years of the same walk, the same pursuit of water and sorghum and nothing more that would follow for the rest of the days of my life, I wept. My body shuddered and heaved as I lay on my back. I crossed my arms over my chest and held my shoulders as I choked back air between sobs. I bit my lower lip and rolled on my side as the tears streamed down my face, dripping off of my nose and into the straw mat beneath me.

XII

Eventually my sobs dried up, and I lay quietly, fighting back the tearless shudders that followed.

As the dry heat evaporated the moisture from my face, I found more tears to replace it.

I have no idea how long I cried, but I know it wasn't long. I lay on my mat and stared up at the grass-thatched roof again. Occasionally, my body would find a bit more moisture and another tear would sprout from the corner of my eye and roll down my cheek. As I lay there in the hot, dry darkness of the hut, I took comfort in stretching my muscles on my mat and wondered why I hadn't made a habit sooner of crying myself out each afternoon and lying on my back for a few minutes.

But every time I thought about how nice it was to rest my body, only fourteen years old but already aching from a decade of labor, I remembered that the only reason I was resting was because I was supposed to be preparing dinner and attending to the household, but without any water, I was incapable of doing either.

It would still be a while before my father came home. It would still be a while before he caught me lying on my mat, doing nothing, before he found out that I had no water, had no water jar, and had no plan.

I thought back over my years and tried to remember my easiest day. The comfort of my sleeping mat made me think that perhaps I was enjoying my easiest day, but then I remembered that I had walked twice for water that day, and had lost my water jar when those men...

Then I remembered. Eight years ago, the day my mother was buried, I was six years old. For one day, there was no water to fetch, there was no house to clean and repair. There was no firewood to gather. For one day, I sat next to my mother's cold body and the people of the village brought us cool cups of water and pots of grain and curry—a tomato sauce curry with chicken in it no less. I sat next to her body, wrapped up before it was taken away and I cried into my bowl of turmeric rice and curry. My chest shuddered and heaved as a I drank the water.

The mourners each stopped by with their gifts and nodded to my father. The women gently placed their hands on my forehead as they passed by.

I remember Uncle Raj bent down, lifted up my chin and told me, "She will be with us again, she is here already," and he smiled.

But it only made me cry harder, and I sobbed and ran inside the hut. I laid down on my sleeping mat, stared up at the grass-thatched roof and cried, the heat evaporating the tears from my cheeks.

Yesterday, as I lay on my mat and stared at the ceiling, with the heat and light of the sun tunneling its way through the thatching, I realized that my best days were also my worst days.

I rolled over and faced the wall, and picked at the grass and mud there.

Suddenly, heavy footsteps approached from the roadway. I could recognize my father's footsteps before he was twenty feet away and I sat up and wiped the moisture from my face.

He was home early. I knew he must have heard what happened. The man in the jeep must have went and told him and he came home early to punish me. My breathing accelerated as the footsteps came to a halt outside of the hut.

He threw open the door flap and poked his head inside, straining to see in the darkness after stepping out of the bright sunlight.

"Sejal!" he shouted. "Why are you sitting? Get up! Come now!"

I reluctantly stood up, walked to the door and peaked out. He was already by the roadway.

"Sejal!" he shouted impatiently. "Hurry, come now!"

He walked quickly towards the village center and I ran to catch up, following closely on his heels, skipping to stay close as we walked.

XIII

A large crowd of people had gathered around the spot where the men had been working. My father and I were some of the last to arrive, and as I looked around, I saw that nearly everyone in the entire village was there.

When my father came to the edge of the crowd, he stopped, turned around and looked at me.

"Your face is red and puffy," he said. "Are you sick?"

I simply looked down to the ground and shook my head. He shrugged, and then snaked his way through the crowd to join Uncle Raj near the front. I found Manisha on the outskirts with the other women, and stood silently beside her, watching as a group of men from the city fastened a metal contraption onto the top of the work site and ratcheted down the bolts with wrenches.

Without any theatrics, the men picked up their tools, one of them nodded towards their work truck and they put their tools away. A man, a short, dark-skinned man, slowly but gracefully climbed onto the raised cement platform of the work site, and smiled out at the crowd. It was the man from the jeep, Thomas. His teeth glistened in the sunlight as he smiled and talked and looked out over the crowd of people who had assembled.

The man said several things that I could not hear from the back of the crowd. But the men in the front laughed cordially with him. Suddenly, his voice burst forth over the whole village.

"You know that we came here to drill a well many days ago," he spoke in Marathi, the language of our village.

Several of the men in the front shook their heads, one of them shouted something I could not hear and the others laughed.

"I know," he continued. "I know that the government has come to drill a well for you many times already. Each time, they have left and you have been left walking many kilometers to fetch water for your families and your animals.

"And we too, we drilled in the best place, the place our scientist said, and still we found nothing. Deeper and deeper we drilled, but still we found nothing. Finally, after 500 feet, we stopped and pulled the drill machinery out, and it was wet. But still, we could achieve no water pressure.

"Three times we cleaned out the bore, and three times we found water at the bottom, but no pressure. And so I told my crew to pack up, and we covered the top of the hole with a large stone. The men of your village thought we would never come back, but

I made them a promise, I promised that we would come back in three days.

"For those three days I went back to Bangalore, and I prayed. I prayed to my God and his son Jesus that they would show you that there is only one God, a God who loves all of his children the same—"

Many of the men in the crowd were already shaking their heads, one yelled something and then others followed.

"Will we not see now?" Thomas shouted above the crowd.

"You're damn right we will," one man shouted.

"Indeed," Thomas laughed his friendly laugh and his eyes twinkled as he looked over the crowd. "If today there is water— water where no one else can achieve it—you will know that it is because there is one true God. It is not a magic trick, it is because He is real and powerful, and because He loves you. It is because my friends and I, in Bangalore and around the world, have prayed for you and brought money and tools and workers to Muthura-mapuram because we love you as God loves you."

The crowd was growing restless, and I hoped for the sake of the man who had saved me earlier that there would be water in the well. The men shifted their feet and grimaced, and some of them clenched their hands into fists as they watched the man talk about his "God." I hoped with everything inside of me that he would do something and water would pour out and he could get back into his jeep and drive back to Bangalore.

But Thomas took his time as he walked back towards the contraption. He explained to the men in the front how the pump mechanism worked.

From where I was standing, it seemed that he muttered to himself as he reached for the handle, but whatever he was saying quietly, it only made the men in the front clench their fists tighter and shift their weight from side to side.

The man lifted up on the handle, and then pushed it back down. Other than the squeaking of the metal handle against the mechanism, there was no sound. He continued to mutter to himself, and he worked the handle again.

The crowd seemed to inch closer, and again he drew the handle up, and then pushed it back down. My stomach burned as I watched, hoping with all of my strength and all of my spirit that water would come out.

I felt nauseous as a chuckle began in the front of the crowd, and the laughter spread out over the assembly.

Thomas wiped his brow, and once again raised the handle. I looked to the ground and covered my eyes with my hands, I couldn't bear to watch. But as he lowered the handle, instead of the squeaking of metal against metal, the sound of rushing water burst forth from the spout. Water splattered to the cement pad the men had built. I looked up and saw that Thomas was smiling.

He pumped again and the jeering and chatter stopped as more water rushed out and ran over the cement, trickling off the sides. The village was struck with silence as the water pooled in the dirt around the structure and seeped into the cracked earth.

"Hallelujah," Thomas said to himself again and again as he looked towards the sky. "Hallelujah."

I did not know what the word meant, and I had never heard it before, but as he said it, I knew that it described the hope I had wished inside of me at that moment.

XIV

My anxieties were not long relieved. No sooner had Thomas reclaimed the crowd and explained that the water was for everyone and belonged to no one when he called "Sejal."

Icy sweat ran down my back as he looked directly at me and spoke. "Today I met a young woman in your village, a woman who has fetched water her whole life."

I wanted to melt away, to seep into the cracked and dusty earth like the water had. The eyes of the crowd roamed amongst each other, every set of eyes looking for me. I stared at the ground and began to hope again, this time wishing it was all a bad dream that would end soon, so that I could get up and begin the trek towards water.

"Sejal," he called to me. "Sejal, will you come up here?"

The crowd in front of me parted to form a pathway to the front. I shook my head 'no' but Manisha gave me a shove from behind.

"Perfect! Manisha, you can come up too!" I looked behind me and her eyes widened and she shook her head, but soon enough we were moving together towards the front, holding hands.

Uncle Raj's hand was on his forehead and my father's eyes burned questions into my brain as I passed him, but still Manisha and I continued toward the man.

"Sejal," the man spoke to me loud enough for others to hear once I reached the front. "I am so impressed by you. God loves you, as he loves all his children, but though you are still just a girl, you work for your family every day. I want you to have something."

He motioned to a man, who brought up a brand new, bright green plastic water jug. Thomas took it from him, and then handed it to me.

"This water is for everyone," he explained. "This jar is green, the color of new life. We were told this ground was cursed. But now we have water."

Then he leaned forward and whispered to me, "there is a God who is more powerful than every curse."

Thomas stepped back to the pump, and then he asked me "Sejal, will you fill your jar with this new water?"

I nodded, "thank you sir," I whispered, though I am certain no one heard. I walked to the spout and the man worked the pump.

I heard the most beautiful sound, the sound of water pouring from above into a plastic water jar. Suddenly, my anxiety was broken, the tension in my shoulders dissipated, and as the water splashed off the rim of the plastic jar and onto my sari, I giggled. I laughed as my jar was filled with this new water.

The man stopped pumping when the jar was full, and tears ran down my cheeks to mix with the water on my sari.

I turned around to face the crowd. I looked out at them and I smiled. Never before had I seen so many friendly faces. The men in the front bowed their heads just slightly and the women in the back smiled openly, nodding their heads.

I looked to my father. My Uncle Raj held his hand, and my father's eyes glistened. For the first time I can remember, I saw his teeth, lips open in a wide smile.

XV

Today I sit on my rock. I sit here because yesterday was a different day than I have ever seen before.

After Thomas filled my jar, he gave Manisha one too, which she accepted gratefully and filled. As the crowd began to disperse, a man who had worked on the well came and talked to the young women huddled in the back. He reminded us that we could go to the government school in our village whenever we wanted, and he also told us about a sewing school in Bangalore, run by the people who had drilled the well. He told us that since we didn't have to fetch water anymore, we might have time to learn a new trade to make money for our families.

I stood behind my father and listened to another of the city men tell them about irrigation. He said that with the water pressure readings, our village could irrigate more than ten acres of land for vegetables, as well as raise more chickens and livestock.

I will think about schools and irrigation and livestock and trades tomorrow. This morning I washed my sari, and I washed myself behind the hut. I've never washed my body this close to my own home before.

This morning, the women of the village stood by the well and chatted as we filled our jars, one by one. For forty minutes we stood leisurely by and waited, then each of us went to our homes, hours before we would have walked in from fetching water from the stream. For the first time in our lives, we returned our water jars to our homes and for the first time ever we were filled with more energy upon returning home than we woke up with.

Now, I sit on this rock and sip my water. As I look up at the clouds, I think of my mother, and I imagine that she is here with us somewhere. I imagine that she looks at me, and her hand glides gently over my braids.

"Ninnie babba ninnie," she sings. She smiles, because she knows that the curse is broken.

About the Story

Although the character of Sejal is fictional, there are literally a billion women around the world that face struggles just like hers, every day. While the dangers vary by region, almost all of them deal with the constant threat of abduction, wild animals, injury and, worst of all, unclean water for their families.

The town of Muthuramapuram is a real place in India, and Thomas is based on a real person, our dear friend Pastor A. Stephen who passed away in 2012. In 2009, my wife Melissa and I had the privilege of saving our money and, with Pastor Stephen's help, drilled a well in this remote Hindu village. Although the specific characters and events are fictional, the story of the well drilling itself is based on Pastor Stephen's account of the well he drilled on our behalf in Muthuramapuram.

There are thousands more villages just like this one that need clean drinking water. Nothing will change the lives of these women and these families more in a single day than access to abundant clean water.

Not only will it change their lives in a single day, but it's something that they can't provide for themselves. It's virtually impossible for villages populated by uneducated, unskilled workers to ever save enough money to provide clean water resources for themselves. And as long as the lives of women and children are dedicated to finding and fetching water, they'll never have the opportunity for education or skill development to be able to change that.

But this is a problem that we can solve. While the thought of providing clean water for everyone in the world might seem staggering, in most areas a well can be drilled for $4 to $10 per villager. Even if we only solve the problem a few hundred families at a time, those are real people, real young women, real Sejals who will wake up the next morning with radically different lives, and radically different opportunities.

Please get involved on a personal level. Find a group that you trust, and make something happen. There are real Sejals in the world, and with your help, tomorrow can be radically, amazingly different.

The women of Muthuramapuram fetching water from their well.

The village of Muthuramapuram, India.

Pastor Stephen (Thomas) stands third from the right.

In 2011, Brad and Melissa Pauquette founded The Water Cycle Project, an organization which provides fresh water wells to remote villages in rural India. As a zero-overhead organization, every dollar raised goes directly to drilling wells.

Learn more and consider donating at
www.WaterCycleProject.org

Afterword
Tom Pauquette

Water - such an easy word to say and easy to obtain for most of us reading these words. Yet water is a daily struggle for hundreds of millions of people around the world. Every 20 seconds in developing countries a child under five years of age dies from preventable water borne diseases.

Brad Pauquette met Pastor A. Stephen, an Indian man, when he was nine years old. Pastor Stephen was a guest speaker at a church during a visit to the United States. Brad was in a local AWANA program at the time and needed a signature from a missionary. On that day a lifelong friendship was born. Today Brad is a grown man and Pastor Stephen has passed away, but the bond that was forged between them through many years of friendship will always exist.

Pastor Stephen had a passionate love for his people of India and worked tirelessly to bring them the good news of Jesus and to alleviate suffering. One of his passions was well drilling to bring clean drinking water to remote villages in south central India.

Sejal is a vivid picture of life for many women and girls in India. As you read this story let it seep into your heart and mind. This story has been written by a man whose heart has been to India even though his feet have never touched its soil. Please share this story with your family, friends, neighbors and coworkers. We can change the world with the love of Jesus one drop at a time.

Tom Pauquette is the pastor of Vineyard Christian Fellowship in Grove City, Ohio.

Acknowledgments

Thank you to all of the people who helped with the production of this book.

Thank you to Amy S. Dalrymple, friend and fellow writer, who generously provided her copy editing services.

Thank you to Benjamin Howes for his help with the cover artwork, and to Emily Hitchcock for proofreading.

Thank you to my mother, Karen Pauquette, for prompting the production of a print version of this book, and for her help with The Water Cycle Project.

Thank you to the members of Columbus Creative Cooperative who provided valuable feedback on the first drafts of this story and helped me to improve it.

Thank you to all of the people who have generously donated money to The Water Cycle Project, to drill wells in India for people that need them. You inspire me every day with your selflessness.

And finally, thank you to the Spirit, who helped me to spend time in a place that I've never visited, and who helped me to see, touch and feel the fields of rural India from a world away.

About the Author

Brad Pauquette is a writer living in Columbus, Ohio. He currently pays the bills by working as an independent web developer.

He is the director and founder of Columbus Creative Cooperative, an Ohio writers' resource, and Columbus Press, an independent publisher.

He is currently rehabbing a home in an inner-city neighborhood of Columbus, where he lives with his wife, Melissa, and their two sons.

In 2011, Brad rode his bike across Ohio as part of The Water Cycle Project (www.WaterCycleProject.org), an organization that raises money to drill fresh water wells in India.

Brad is a follower of Jesus. He believes that it's important and necessary to depict the troubled world around him realistically in his writing.

Brad does his best to answer all emails. You can reach him at bradpauquette@gmail.com, or by U.S. Mail at Brad Pauquette, P.O. Box 91028, Columbus, OH 43209.

You can learn more about Brad at BradPauquette.com.